# The Berenstain Bears® and the BIG RED KITE

Stan & Jan Berenstain

Reader's Digest Kids

Westport, Connecticut


Published by Reader's Digest Young Families, Inc. Printed in the U.S.A.

ISBN: 0-89577-731-2

Look, Sister Bear!
Hooray! Hooray!
The big kite contest
is today!

Yes, Brother Bear.
I see. That's right.
But we can't go.
We have no kite!

No kite? No kite?
Now, do not worry.
I can make one
in a hurry!

A kite for Sister Bear and me?

I'll make a kite.

Just wait and see.

First some sticks—
just two will do.
Some paper, string,
and a little glue.

We tie.
We cut.
Now, we glue.
See? I made a kite
for you!

A big red kite!

It's a beauty!

Big Red Kite,

do your duty!

It sure is red.
No doubt about it.
But will it fly?
I really doubt it.

For, you see,
without a tail,
that big red kite
is sure to fail.

This old bedsheet
will make a tail.

This tail will help
Big Red to sail.

Kite contest,
we're on our way!
Our big red kite
will win the day!

Kites! Kites!
Up ahead!

Look out, kites.

Here comes Big Red!

Kites of every
shape and size
sail and dance
across the skies—

box kite,

fox kite,

kite with eyes,

kites that look like butterflies,

a dragon with
a long green tail,

a kite that says:
SAVE THE WHALE.

The judge looks
down his nose at Red.
“It looks homemade,”
the kite judge said.

Other unkind things are said:

Oh? Oh?
Is that so?
It's time to fly!
Here we go!

Run, Papa! Run!

Do your stuff!

There is some wind,

but not enough!

JUDGE

We won't give up!
We'll keep on trying.
Red will soon
be up and flying!

Look, Papa! Look!
The wind grows strong!

In wind like this,
those fancy kites
will not last long!

Look! Red flies high,
and higher still!

I know we'll win!
I know we will!

SAVE
THE

That wind is strong.
That wind is rough.
Those other kites
weren't strong enough!

Big Red has won
fair and square.
Congratulations,
Papa Bear!

We won! We won,

Mama Bear!

Our big red kite

won fair and square!

You passed a more
important test:
You didn't quit!
You did your best.